D.P.

WESTERN A

W

THE BANDIT
OF THE BLACK HILLS

MAX BRAND

THE BANDIT
OF THE BLACK HILLS

G.K.HALL &CO.
Boston, Massachusetts
1991

Published in Large Print by arrangement with
G. P. Putnam's Sons.

British Commonwealth rights courtesy of A.M. Heath & Co. Limited.

G. K. Hall Large Print Book Series.

Set in 18 pt. Plantin.

Library of Congress Cataloging-in-Publication Data

Brand, Max, 1892-1944.
    The bandit of the Black Hills / Max Brand.
        p.   cm.—(G.K. Hall large print book series)
    ISBN 0-8161-5078-8 (lg. print)
    1. Large type books.   I. Title.
[PS3511.A87B3   1991]
813'.52—dc20
                                                         90-45901

THE BANDIT
OF THE BLACK HILLS

Back to Wheeler City

WHEN THEY HEARD that The Duke was coming back, they gathered from all quarters. Charlie Barr dropped into Wheeler City from Northern Montana. Old man Minter came in from New Mexico near the line. Bill Thunder, of Big Bend fame, got off the train in time to shake hands with Harry Matthews from Spokane. The four were perhaps the most famous of those who came to Wheeler City, but there were others who arrived, one by one, unheralded and unsung, grim-faced men with guns in working order and a sacred purpose of ridding the earth of that celebrated encumbrance, The Duke.

They filled Wheeler City with sleepless nights. Not that they went about proclaiming their intentions from the housetops or at midnight. That was by no means true of them, for they were, on the whole, quiet-spoken, gentle-acting men. And they had come on such a serious mission that much noise was not in order. Men needed quiet so that nerves and brains would be prepared for the sudden test.

And the result was that a terrible silence fell upon Wheeler City. Even during the day men moved about with soft footfalls, and when Sam Curtin, the huge butcher, came in to gossip with old Jake Deland, the hotel proprietor, he talked in a whisper, glancing secretly about him and over his shoulder while he talked.

What was the sheriff's opinion? The sheriff was an old man and a wise man. He bore the weird and unsavory name of Onion. And the cunning of Tom Onion was celebrated afar.

Of course he was consulted by timorous townsfolk. He was asked what he would do. His response was to ask the townsfolk what he could do. And when they went on to say that, if something were not done, there would be a killing when The Duke returned to town, he replied that they were perfectly right, saying that the word "killing" should be put into the plural. Men were certain to die.

The logic of the sheriff was unimpeachable. His attitude might have seemed more questionable. Sheriffs were supposed to do their best to prevent crime, and Tom Onion seemed to be shirking his sworn duty. To balance that opinion there were ten years of fearless and diligent service of the public to the credit of the sheriff. No matter how he talked it was known that his actions would be greater than his words.

But what the sheriff said, most briefly reported, was simply this: The Duke is a killer. We all admit that he is. The longer he lives, the more people he'll kill. He has the taste, the style, the speed and the surety of a natural man-slayer. Sooner or later he must be removed for the safety of society. And the sooner he is removed, the better. I myself am willing to face this celebrated fighter, but I confess I am very glad to have such support. Here we have expert guntoters from the far corners of the fighting West. What could be better? All of these men realize that sooner or later The Duke must be removed from the books—wiped out—erased. They are willing to do the erasing. And if one of them meets The Duke there will be an explosion. It is true that The Duke is just out of prison, and that his name is supposed to be clear at the present moment; but we all know that that's supposing a great deal too much!

Such was the reasoning of the wily sheriff. And more than one other man in Wheeler City agreed with him. The Duke was known to be heading home, and it was well to meet him at the entrance to his old home town with guns well oiled and minds resolved on action.

And The Duke himself?

He detached himself from beneath a freight car when the train slowed to a crawl at the steep grade three miles out of town. From that point The Duke walked in. Why should The Duke, who hated physical exertion of all kinds, and walking above all the rest—why should The Duke walk into Wheeler City?

A foreboding had come to him through the empty air that it would be well to enter Wheeler City softly and without a blare of brass to herald his coming. So The Duke walked in. Neither did he aim straight for the heart of town, though his very vitals had ached with desire to see that place during the three years of his absence. But rather he chose to stalk along the outskirts. He listened at windows and near open doors. He picked up a word here and another there in the broken conversations he overheard, and with the matchless shuttle of suspicion he wove them in a solid cloth. In half an hour of lurking here and there he knew that Wheeler City was filled with armed men who were bent on shooting him down at sight.

When he had made out this information The Duke retired to a dark corner where a tall fence walled him away on three sides with shadow. Here he rolled a cigarette and lighted it and smoked it. It would have been well had his enemies been near by to study his face feature by feature. He was smiling. They would have noted that first.

He had always been a great smiler in the old days. And the prison had not changed him. It had rubbed away his tan; it had rubbed away his clear and healthy color. Instead, his face was chalk-white, so that the straight black brows were the more pronounced. They met like a deep marking of soot straight across his forehead. And beneath them the eyes glittered and went out from time to time like a covered lantern behind its shutter.

And the young men of Wheeler City would have noticed that The Duke was not less good-looking, just as the old men of Wheeler City would have noticed that three years of hard labor in the State penitentiary had not given him a hangdog manner. His spirit was not broken. That, after all, was to be expected. For they had actually cut short his term on account of good behavior.

Good behavior on the part of The Duke!

However, the world could not be expected to know The Duke as Wheeler City knew him. And when the glow of the cigarette illumined The Duke's smile, the world could not be expected to know that Wheeler City dreaded that particular sort of smile, with the white teeth showing, more than it dreaded The Duke's frown.

He finished the cigarette down to a small butt. Then he dropped it, ground it carefully under his heel, rose and stretched every muscle in his six-feet-one of length. In this fashion a cat, which has been drowsing by the fire through the evening, rises, stretches, makes sure of its strength, and then, with silent footfalls, steals out into the black night to hunt. And as it unsheathes its claws from their cushions of silk, so The Duke unsheathed his six-shooter, weighed it lightly in his long fingers and then stowed it away again.

Having done this, he went straight to the sheriff's house. He went there because the town would least expect to find him in that place, and therefore it would be safest. He went there also because, of all things, The Duke most dearly loved to do the unexpected.

When he reached the dwelling, a brief survey through the windows convinced him that the sheriff was not at home. The sheriff's wife and his two daughters were finishing the supper dishes in the kitchen. So The Duke went around to the veranda and opened the window of the sheriff's office. He stepped inside, sat down in a comfortable chair in the corner behind the filing cabinet, folded his hands in his lap, leaned his head against the wall, and closed his eyes. For he knew that with the eyes shut one's senses are far more alert and acute in the blackness of night. Also, he wanted to think.

His thoughts were a swift survey of his life. He began with the time when he had been a nameless, fatherless, motherless foundling, drifting here and there, picking up a living at the age of eight by doing chores. He followed the course of his life until, a little past adolescence, he had discovered two things: First, that work was mortally distasteful; second, that he had qualities which set him apart from his fellow men.

It is dangerous enough at any period of

life for a man to learn that he is more blessed in certain God-given essentials than are his companions. But it is trebly dangerous when the discovery is made in childhood. And at the green age of fourteen, The Duke acquired both his strange nickname and his reputation. He got his name on account of his careless scorn of even the most formidable ruffians on the wide cattle range where formidable and freedom-loving men are apt to gather. And he got his reputation through his uncanny ability with a gun.

It was not that The Duke was vain of his accomplishment or that he boasted of it or that he cherished his attainment with constant practice. But when he drew forth a gun it seemed that a tightened string ran from its muzzle to the target he wished to strike. Just as some men are born with great speed in their legs and others are born with a keen taste for sweets and sours, so The Duke was born with an eye which looked straight and with nerves which could not tremble. One is not vain of such inborn accomplishments any more than one is vain of a gold mine which one has stumbled upon by chance. But just as one is sure to dig out the gold and spend it, so The Duke could not avoid exploiting his powers.

There followed three years of riotous adventure and wild living. He roamed from Alaska to the City of Mexico, and wherever he went he stayed only long enough to build up a fame which caused brave men to avoid him. Then he went on to fresh fields and pastures new to find untried foemen. He did not cling to gunwork only. If it were a matter of fisticuffs, at sixteen he had the strength of a grown man and the natural speed of a wildcat. In the winter of his seventeenth year he lived in lumber camps in Canada and passed through a graduate school in rough-and-tumble fighting. And the following spring and summer he was initiated into the intricate mysteries of a profession of which he already knew the ABC's and the simple grammar—knife play.

And still, no matter where he went and no matter what he did, he was forgiven. For he was "only a boy." And if a boy wanted to fight grown men it was the fault of the men if they were injured. Surely no jury could convict him.

There was a sudden change, however, in his eighteenth year. He had had his full height now for two years, and for two years he had been broadening and hardening into the full strength and the full bearing of manhood. At seventeen he had looked nineteen or twenty. At eighteen, a scant year later, he looked all of twenty-four.

And in the West a man is a man at twenty-four. The Duke discovered it to his cost on a day in New Mexico when he fell into an argument with three stalwart Mexicans and settled the dispute with his gun. It did not matter afterward that he offered to pay the funeral expenses of the dead man and the hospital bills of the other two. He was led to a jail. They starved him on meager fare for a week, and then the sheriff, a mild man, came to him and said he believed the thing might have been mere self-defense, that a jury, however, would hang him, and that he had better get out. So that night he dug a hole through the wall and escaped.

The next lesson was in the State of Washington. For a little exercise one evening he found that he had all the grown men of the town riding hard on his heels. He managed to square that account by hunting down that notorious man-killer and robber, Nicolo Baccigalupi, better known by the awful title of "Black Nick." He found Black Nick, challenged him, shot a gun out of his hand and brought the wounded captive into town. And for that deed he was pardoned the wounds he had dealt two days before and allowed to go on his way.

But after those first two exploits he came to realize that the world was looking upon him through different eyes. However, it is sometimes easier to see danger than to avoid it. And to The Duke it had been bread and meat. He could not keep his hands out of trouble. He had kicked up ructions for three years and more. And now the horned gentleman was his bunky, so to speak.

What The Duke did in his eighteenth year would have filled several books, until at last, on a hurried excursion back to Wheeler City, he saw the sweet face of Linda Murray. From that moment he decided that he would make Wheeler City his home both in name and in fact. He would settle down. He would no longer strive to get rich at the card table, but by honest labor he would make honest wages, save them, and so earn the means of establishing a home for Linda. And all was smooth before him. Linda was swept from her feet by this hero of eighteen who looked a man full grown, and had about him the aroma of strange deeds and strange lands. If she were a year or two his senior, it did not matter. All went on well enough.

And then came that Saturday night trip

to town from old man Carter's ranch where he was working, the meeting with Springer, the interplay of jests, the sudden hard words, the shooting.

The thoughts of The Duke vanished. The front door of the sheriff's house had opened, and footfalls and voices were sounding in the hall.

2

Guthrie's Madman

THIS WAS ALL extremely awkward. He had planned on meeting the sheriff alone. But if he encountered two men they were both apt to start shooting without asking for explanations of why he was waiting for them there in that darkened room. He would have tried to slip away through the window, but if they opened the door and saw the silhouette of a man escaping through the window they would unquestionably fill him full of lead. So he got up from his chair, backed into the corner behind the filing cabinet, and saw that his revolver was in readiness. Then he waited.

The door to the office opened. The two

voices mumbled to a pause as the speakers stepped into the blackness. Then a match was scratched, and The Duke saw the pale light waver across the ceiling with its net-work of deep cracks and fissures. A lamp was lighted, and the glow of it, as the flame settled in the circular burner, seemed to The Duke as bright as the sun of midday. Where would they sit down? No matter where, one of them was sure to see him. And then the explosion!

But: "I ain't going to sit down, Sheriff," said the voice of the stranger.

"All right, Mr. Guthrie. If you're pressed for time—"

"I'm making it back to the ranch tonight."

"Tonight!"

"Yes, sir."

"Thirty miles by buckboard in the dark on those roads?"

"If the hosses will stand it, I'll stand it, Sheriff Onion."

"You know your own business, Mr. Guthrie."

"I don't know my own business. Otherwise I wouldn't be here. All I know is that some murdering hound up in the Black Hills has been using my ranch as a sort of general merchandise store for the past two years, and when I got tired of having things stole out of my saddle room or out of my pantry, and when I started to get my punchers together and send 'em out to trail him down, he pays me back by slipping down out of his hills and trying to murder me!"

"The devil!" said the sheriff.

"That's putting it mild!"

"I've heard that yarn about the man in the Black Hills. Matter of fact, we've all heard about him. And I have my explanation. When you told me about it first, I tried to explain—"

"I know," broke in Guthrie impatiently. "You tried to explain by saying that there wasn't any one man in the Black Hills, but that it was a sort of stopping place for long riders and scamps of one sort and another on their way across country, and that the reason they all picked on me was because my ranch was the only one near to the hills. That's the way you talked then."

"And I still say the same thing. I'll tell you why I know. If there were one man living all the time in the Black Hills, I'd of come across his sign when I was hunting him there, and I've hunted the Black Hills four times to get at this ghost robber of yours, Guthrie."

"That proves nothing."

The sheriff flushed. He was a known trailer. "Maybe not. Maybe it don't mean much. But I've spent a solid month in the Black Hills. I've trailed 'em from bottom to the top. I've gone over 'em with a microscope, you might say. And I ain't seen signs that are more than just here and there. There ain't any trails of the kind a man would make if he was living there all the time. Another thing, Guthrie. If he was up there regular, wouldn't he be riding down here all the time and cleaning up in Wheeler City and all the other towns around the Black Hills?"

There was a grunt from Guthrie.

"I dunno about that," he said. "All I know is that the same gent is the one that's doing the work out to my ranch."

"What proof have you got?" asked the sheriff wearily.

"The way he does things."

"Well?"

"And the fact that he's been seen!"

"You saw him two years ago." The sheriff yawned, manifestly weary of this profitless and stubborn talk. "You got on the trail of somebody that had stole a side of bacon, and you and your boys rode till you come in sight

15

of a gent on a pinto. You see that gent about half a mile away, I figure!"

"Closer'n that."

"Not close enough for shooting."

"Close enough to see his long hair and to see that it was black and that he was not more'n twenty-five. Nope, he was a pile younger'n that."

"Well," said the sheriff, suppressing a chuckle, "you figure that this same gent is still doing the raiding?"

"I do that."

"What's your evidence?"

"I seen him yesterday not a hundred feet away!"

"The devil!" gasped the sheriff, his indifference quite gone.

"It was worse'n the devil."

"A hundred feet away?"

"With light in his face!"

"Guthrie, this is important. What did he look like?"

"Like he hadn't got no older in these two years. He had the same long black hair. Didn't look much older'n a kid. Fine-looking, sort of. But good looks don't make a good man!"

"Not by some miles they don't! Ain't The Duke the handsomest boy you ever seen?"

"He was before my time, but this young mountain rat has the nerve of the devil himself. Lemme tell you what happened! He came down a couple of days ago and tried to raid me, but one of my punchers seen him. He raised a yell and he started after this gent. The man from the Black Hills lighted out for the Black Hills. They got close enough to him to see that he could ride like the devil, but he ducked away from them, and they lost the trail. Which I got sort of mad and had a talk with my nephew Steve. Steve and me figured it would be pretty good to lay for this robber. We done it yesterday, and we pretty near caught him coming down out of the hills about twilight. If there'd been bright sun we'd of filled him full of lead and salted him away for keeps. But the dull light bothered us, and this outlaw rode his pinto like a snipe flying. He dodged across country, and when we seen we'd missed him and tried to ride him down, he had enough of a lead. He cut back into the hills and seemed to just melt away into the solid rock.

"But it must of sort of riled him to have me follow him up that way. He came down last night and shot at me through the win-

17

dow. The slug chipped off a chunk of hair above my ear!"

"The murdering hound!" growled the sheriff. "There ought to be a law to burn a sneak alive."

"I grabbed a gun and cut for the outside. When I come out I seen the young hound standing—where would you think?"

"Can't guess, Guthrie."

"Right by the window of the bunkhouse. That was how I seen him so clear. The lamplight was shining through on him—and he was laughing!"

"But didn't you have a gun?"

"I did, but I ain't the champion shot in the world, and he must have knowed it. He was rolling a cigarette, I think. I ups with my gun and blazes away. Hanged if he didn't keep standing there a second right in the light—to finish his cigarette, I guess—and finally he just strolled around the corner of the bunkhouse!"

"Where were your punchers?"

"They came tearing out of the bunkhouse. I tried to holler to them to run around behind the bunkhouse and they'd catch the man I wanted. But they had heard the shooting. The slugs I'd fired at the thief had whacked right through the walls of the house. They all were shouting to one another, and they didn't hear me. Doggone me if the fools didn't start running to get hosses—like as if they couldn't even think till they'd got into saddles. And by the time they got all ready and on their hosses, of course the killer was clean gone. We trailed him this morning, though. He'd come right up behind the bunkhouse. He'd left his hoss there. Then he'd gone exploring. We follered his sign clear back to the Black Hills, but we lost the trail in the rocks there. And that's why I'm here, Sheriff. I'll be a dead man inside of a week if I don't get some sort of protection!"

"Guthrie," said the sheriff, "this is sure a queer yarn, but you're going to get protection. Kind of gives me the creeps just to think of this! There's only one explanation —you're right and I'm wrong. And there's only one kind of gent that would fire through a window at you and then stand off and laugh at you and your gun as you come out."

"What do you mean?"

"Don't you understand? The fellow's insane!"

"A crazy man!" gasped Guthrie. "By the Lord, Sheriff, you're right. But it's sure going to take all the nerve out of me to go back and face that sort of music!"

"How about the punchers?"

"They're getting plumb nervous. An old hand quit and come in with me in the buckboard this morning. And after he'd told his story around I couldn't get nobody to take his place."

"That's hard luck, Guthrie. How about your nephew?"

"He stands it fine. There ain't such a thing as fear in Steve. When I was young I had a pretty steady nerve myself, but it sort of oozes out of a man when he gets along in years. But Steve will stay by me through thick and thin. Pray Heaven this crazy man-killer don't get Steve instead of me!"

His voice shook with emotion.

"Guthrie," said the sheriff gently, "I'd like to go out and stay on your ranch myself, but you know the trouble I'm going to have with The Duke. I'm needed here on the firing line. But I'll get some sort of protection out to you."

"The sooner the quicker, Sheriff."

"The sooner the quicker. Keep your head up. Maybe you'll never see the young rat again, anyhow."

There was a dubious groan from the rancher, and his heavy footfall left the room. The sheriff closed the door behind him. Already the problem of the rancher had left his mind. So accustomed was he to dealing with the terrors and the sorrows of other men that he was actually humming as he stepped back toward his desk. And this was the moment The Duke chose to step out from his place of concealment.

3

The Duke Dispels a Doubt

IT WAS A rude shock for the sheriff. His eyes rolled wildly, as though he were unable to choose between earthly or ghostly fear and identify his visitor. But presently, gray of face, shaky of voice, he said: "The Duke!"

"That same," said The Duke cheerfully.

The sheriff shrugged his shoulders to gather his nerve. He advanced with hand outstretched. He forced a wan smile to curve his lips.

"John Morrow," he said, "no matter what men have held against you, you are now a clean man in the eyes of the law. I'm glad to welcome you back, and I only hope that you stay here in peace."

His unregarded hand fell to his side. The

Duke was looking him in the eyes with that strangely mortifying scorn and quiet contempt which had won him his name. The sheriff drew back a little with a troubled frown.

"I'm wrong about your intentions then, Morrow?"

The Duke smiled upon him and displayed an even line of teeth, flashing white—as scrupulously cared for as the tapering tips of The Duke's fingers, with which he made his living at cards.

"Never wrong about me, Sheriff," said The Duke. "I ain't here looking for no disturbance. I'm a peace-keeper."

The sheriff maintained as solemn a face as possible and nodded.

"No matter how hard I try," said The Duke, "there's going to be somebody around to spoil the sleep for me and the rest of the town. Don't it look that way?"

The sheriff avoided answer by making a cigarette.

"Sit down," he said when The Duke had refused the "makings."

The Duke took the suggested chair and drew it into the farther corner. There he sat down, with no possibility of anything coming behind him or of anyone looking in upon him through the window. The sheriff had observed these maneuvers' with the keenest attention. And suddenly he said, as he sank into a chair facing that of The Duke, "Morrow, how old are you?"

"It doesn't peeve me none to have folks call me Duke," said the latter carelessly. "You don't have to think up that Morrow name. How old am I? I'm old enough to vote."

"I guess you're that old," and the sheriff grinned.

"I was twenty-one last May," said The Duke.

The sheriff thought a moment. "By heavens, it's true!"

"That's sort of mild cussing for you, Sheriff," said The Duke.

"It is," said the other. "But—Duke, how many lifetimes have you crammed into the past seven years?"

"Into the past four years, you mean," said The Duke. "These three just behind me I haven't been living."

He smiled upon the sheriff in such a way that the latter hastily puffed on his cigarette and threw up a smoke screen between himself and his companion. He felt a little more easy behind that false shelter.

"As bad as that?" he said. "Why, I thought that they treated you pretty good down yonder. Didn't they chop a whole year of your term?"

"Sure. The warden got me pardoned," said The Duke. "But you can't be treated well inside of a prison. Stones ain't got the sort of conversation that cheers a man up."

The sheriff shrugged himself into a more comfortable position.

"I guess that's right," he said. "And on you, after being free all your life more'n the average man was free, I guess it was a mite extra hard."

"I boiled down thirty years inside the three," said The Duke calmly. "That's all it meant."

He leaned forward. He took off his hat.

"Look at me," he said as his head came close into the bright circle of the lamplight.

The sheriff looked, and what he saw amazed him. There was a thick sprinkling of gray in the black hair of The Duke. And now that his face was so close to the light he could see that many years had been stamped into the features and the expression. It was enough to make him shudder. And then, sitting back in his chair once more, he drew a great breath and cleared his throat. This interview was beginning to get on his nerves. What did The Duke want with him? Why this continued gentleness? Where was the old insolent, high-handed manner? Where was the flashing eye, the ready sneer, the cutting words? Truly The Duke had changed miraculously. Only his smile was the same—mirthless, cruel, slow.

"I wanted you to see that," said The Duke, "so's you could understand something."

"I'm listening, Duke."

"I want to quit."

"Eh?"

"I'm through with the game, Sheriff. I want to start in being plumb peaceful."

The sheriff nodded.

"I hope you have luck, Duke."

"You don't think I mean it then? Or you think I can't stick to the resolution? Sheriff, I'm more changed inside than I show in the face, even!"

"You are?"

Here the sheriff sat up with a little more assurance and looked at his terrible visitor more closely. Was it not possible, indeed, that the claws of the lion had been clipped and his teeth drawn?

"I'm all changed," said The Duke.

"I sure hope so. Are you going back to the Carter ranch?"

"I'm going to see Linda first," said the man from prison. He raised his head and smiled. "I sure want to see Linda!" He looked down at the sheriff. "I'll let her tell me what's next best to do."

He found that the sheriff was rubbing his jaw and looking vacantly at him.

"You ain't stopped being fond of that girl, eh?"

"Of course not." He rose suddenly from his chair. His voice changed. "Why should I be?" he demanded.

"No reason," breathed the sheriff as though a gun had been shoved under his nose. "No reason at all—I guess!"

"Partner," said The Duke, all his nonchalance completely gone and his face white and drawn with emotion, "you got something to tell me!"

"Nothing, Duke," said the wretched sheriff, wrung by both pity and dread.

"Sheriff, I've got to have it out of you!"

"You were away too long, Duke."

"And she's married another man!"

"Not that."

"She's engaged then?"

The sheriff nodded, and The Duke

26

stepped back from him, back into the shadow near the wall. Whether he was more struck to the heart by true disappointment such as any lover might feel, or whether he was more tortured by a sense of injured vanity, the sheriff could not decide. But when The Duke stepped a little closer again so that his face could be seen quite clearly, he had controlled his expression. The half-cynical, half-contemptuous smile which was now habitual on his face was playing there again.

"I might of known," he said. "Which a girl is sure to get lonely inside of three years. But who's the man, Sheriff?"

No matter how smooth and purring the voice of The Duke, the sheriff knew that there was danger ahead.

"Don't make much difference, does it? Nobody tried to knife you while your back was turned, Duke."

"No?"

That drawling, queried monosyllable made the sheriff shiver as though ice had been trailed up and down his spine.

"It just happened. Time makes a lot of difference with a young girl, Duke. Besides—"

"Besides, it would have been sort of hard

on her to have anything to do with a jail-bird."

"I didn't say that."

"Then I read your mind, Sheriff. But who's the man?"

"Duke, you ain't going to start on his trail?"

"And get back inside the prison again?" The Duke laughed in a singular and mirth-less manner. "I ain't a fool. If I ever do anything from this time on, it'll be things that the law can't lay a hand on me for. Oh, I've learned my lesson. But I'm curious. Who's the man that got pretty Linda Murray?"

Something in his way of saying "pretty Linda Murray" was proof that in the past ten seconds he had thrust all thought of the girl—at least all hope of her—out of his life forever. And the thought of the cruelly controlled will power which must have been used to bring about such a result made the sheriff sweat with wonder.

"You'd find out sooner or later. It's a gent that you already ain't got much use for. It's Bud Springer, Duke!"

He waited anxiously. But presently The Duke broke into hearty laughter. The sound of that laughter was not audible beyond the room in which they were sitting, but the force of it shook his body.

"That's what I call a pretty good joke," said The Duke. "The gent that I get sent to jail for shooting is the same gent that gets my girl while I'm away!"

And he smiled again, but his face was a sickly color.

"Linda must have been sure fond of me," he commented, "to pick up with that—"

"She was sorry for Bud. You—see—"

"Let's stop talking about her," said The Duke dryly. "If I left a hoss behind me it would have mourned for me a longer time then she done. And if it was so plumb easy for her to forget all about me I reckon that it will be plumb easy for me to forget all about her. But what I want to know about now is this here reception committee that's so doggone anxious to say 'Welcome Home' to me!"

The sheriff smiled in spite of himself.

"The town ain't exactly full of friends of yours, Duke."

"No, it ain't," agreed The Duke. "Some of 'em have come quite a ways looking for me. What's the meaning of it, Sheriff?"

"Can't you guess?"

"Sure. I know that they've come to sink

a chunk of lead in me if they can. But once upon a time they wouldn't've been so anxious—" He hesitated, at a loss for words.

"Once upon a time," translated the sheriff, "they would just as soon have put a noose around their necks as come out hunting The Duke. I know, Duke; but while you been away some of the boys have been practicing with their guns. I suppose they figure that they've got a better chance at you."

"It's open season on me, eh? They can any of 'em go for their gats and try to drop me the minute I'm in sight. And him that gets me will only be cheered. No arrest for him! They'd give him a vote of thanks, most like!"

"In the old days," said the sheriff, "didn't you declare open season on everybody else? Did you hold back to think and ponder any? No, Duke, you went out to get into trouble, and you sure enough got there. Who you hurt didn't make no difference to you. Well, when they hear that you're out of prison, everybody that you've ever injured comes up here loaded for bear. There's Bill Thunder —Billy Hancock, you know. He comes up from Big Bend. He allows that when you dropped his brother, young Hal Hancock, four years back, you done it by taking advantage. And there's Charlie Barr come out of Montana way, saying that you done him dirt a long time ago. And there's others come from every direction. Before, they kept still. They sort of figured that there wasn't no hope in trying to stand up agin' you. But now—"

"But now they figure that I'm out of practice?"

"Something like that."

"So they're stepping out and roaring around pretty loud?"

"Duke, the thing for you to do is to forget that you ever lived in this town. Get away from Wheeler City and stay away! There's too many of 'em here!"

"Get away and stay away?" murmured the ex-convict. "And once I'm gone, have it known all over the ranges that I've showed the white feather?"

"Running from a whole crowd ain't showing the white feather, Duke!"

The Duke stiffened to his full height, and he seemed a giant to the sheriff as the latter looked up at him.

"I ain't particular partial to running, Sheriff!" he said.

The sheriff swallowed and said nothing. He had picked up a box of fishhooks and was juggling them in his hand. Suddenly the ex-convict took the little box from the hand of Tom Onion, crossed the room and stuck a row of six hooks from the lowest rim of the window sash. He crossed the room to the farthest side again, walking slowly, very slowly. And the sheriff, amazed and worried, stared from his guest to the hooks in the window. They were tiny, glimmering points of light as the rays from the lamps touched on the gilt. And as The Duke crossed the room he was talking deliberately to the sheriff.

"I'm not leaving the town, Sheriff," he said. "I've come back to Wheeler City plumb peaceable, but not anxious to move. No, sir, I ain't running from town to get away from nobody! The main reason is something that may surprise you to hear. Sheriff, the yarn I told at my trial, and that everybody laughed at, was a true yarn. I didn't shoot Bud Springer in the back. It's true that we had an argument. It's true that we were pretty close to a gun play. But we stayed on the safe side of one. And the reason was that Bud didn't want none of my medicine. But while we was still talking pretty loud somebody fired through the window and dropped Bud. It was some dirty sneak that knew I'd be blamed for what had happened. I picked Bud up. You remember that he didn't accuse me till the next morning? And I tell you that that night somebody had got to Bud and bribed him or persuaded him to put the blame on me. Or maybe Bud had worked it out that if he got rid of me in jail he'd have a better chance with Linda—"

As he spoke these words he whirled on his heel. As he spun, a heavy Colt had glided into his hand. The sheriff made a futile gesture toward his own weapon, then saw it was far too late and sat quiet. But he was not the target for The Duke. The revolver blazed six times in swift succession—reports crowded as close together as the staccato beat of a typewriter.

And all in a second the firing was ended, and the shriek of the sheriff's wife from the kitchen came to them.

"I'm not leaving Wheeler City," said the ex-convict. "I'm here to stay. If any of the boys that have traveled so far to see me are plumb set on finding me, you tell them that I'm going to have a good sleep tonight, and that tomorrow night I'm going to be out to the big dance at Warner's Springs. If they want to see me bad they can find me there. You can give these six fishhooks to the six that want to find me the most!"

So saying, he stepped out of the window just as the opposite door flew open and the sheriff's wife ran in.

4

The Stamp of the Lawbreaker

IT WAS, OF course, impossible for the sheriff to do anything for a time but attempt to soothe and quiet his wife and assure her that he was not suffering from a mortal injury dealt by the gun of an assassin. And when his wife was off his hands there were eager neighbors who flocked in, drawn by the sound of the fusillade.

To the latter the sheriff showed the demonstration. He went to the window sill. He found in it six heads of fishhooks which had been sunk into the wood just at the edge of the sill. But the parts which projected downward, namely, the eye and the slender shaft of the hook, had been blown away, the metal being clipped off cleanly. And in no instance, saving one only, had the bullet touched the wood. In that case there was a light graze funneling the lower surface of the sill.

The sheriff did not draw out the hooks. Instead, he called his good friends to behold the sight. He held the lamp so that they could see better.

"And all six shots fired by lamplight," he explained calmly, "and all the time used up in getting out his gun and firing them six shots was just about the time that it would take an average good hand with a Colt to get out his gat and pump in one placed shot. Yes, friends, I got to admit that The Duke has fallen down in his shooting so's he can't do better than this. Look how he actually cut the wood with one of them six shots!"

The irony of the sheriff was not needed to drive home the point. The crowd saw, understood, and went away abashed to tell the tale to others. And others heard and came to see for themselves. Big Bill Thunder heard the tale and laughed heartily in derision and came to see for himself. And Big Bill Thunder saw, swore reverently under his breath, and retired with a thoughtful look. And others came to behold it. There was Charlie Barr, and Harry Matthews, who had ridden in all the way from Spokane to "get" his man. And old man Minter came and looked and said nothing and departed in silence. And the others came. They rose out of their beds in the hotel and made a hurried pilgrimage.

It was not until midnight that the sheriff's house was silent again. The rest of Wheeler City, meantime, was murmuring. A faint buzz of conversation did not go out with the lamps, and there was a strain of talk here and there until the dawn came and wakened the rest of the town.

Once well awakened, the town heard new tidings passed around, and with the news went great laughter. Terrible old man Minter was gone from Wheeler City for parts unknown. Harry Matthews, who had come all the way from Spokane, had presumably started all the way back again. Charlie Barr was nowhere to be found, and Bill Thunder had presumably felt a sudden passion to see once more the muddy waters of the Rio Grande.

All, all the heroes were gone! And on the field of battle there was left only the solitary form of The Duke. Yes, in the drowsy latter half of the warm July morning The Duke appeared, strolling with the utmost leisure down the street. And, with his accustomed courtesy, he was seen raising his hat to the ladies and bowing to the men.

 . Who had taught The Duke these strangely formal manners? Perhaps he had learned them from some old Mexican gentleman who had about him more of the Spanish than a mere name. Perhaps something was born into The Duke, something of which he himself knew nothing. But at least there was no example for that stately courtesy, that formalism of manners, in Wheeler City or in any of its environs.

So down the street went The Duke, and it seemed to matter nothing to him that the men he encountered stared and grunted in answer to his salutations, and that the women, whether old or young, stared and did not answer at all.

"They been telling yarns about me," said The Duke calmly. "Doggone if they ain't been telling stories about me all the time. They got me eating raw meat by this time."

The thought pleased him so much and seemed so apt that he paused in the middle of a stride and laughed heartily, albeit in silence. That laughter was noted by a little boy who, clinging to the calico skirts of his mother, was passing on the farther side of the street. And he gasped in terror and excitement. That fear in the child was not un-noticed by The Duke. It made his brow black with anger—but in an instant he had smoothed his expression again and had gone smiling on his way.

He reached the hotel. On the veranda he lingered and looked up and down its length as he stood on the middle step, leading in from the street. But not one of the half dozen loungers cared to meet his eye. He strolled to the door of the musty old room which served as a lobby. And there was no violent and sudden stir of angry and courageous men jumping to their feet to open fire on him.

The Duke looked them over one by one with that famous smile of his. Then he turned, paused on the veranda to roll a cig-arette, and, finally, with smoke curling above his head, stepped down to the street and continued on his way.

It was even worse than he had imagined. He had fondly thought that a term served for an offense wipes out the balance against a wrongdoer. Now he saw that society is apt to use a penitentiary merely as a means of putting a brand upon a man by which he may be set apart from the law-abiding during the rest of his mortal days. He had done the spectacular thing. He had routed his enemies before they had a chance to strike a blow at him, but the victory remained with the hostile forces!

He paused in front of the blacksmith shop which Bud Springer operated. He stepped to the door. Instantly there was confusion within. A door opened hastily at the rear of the shop, and a shadowy form, screened by the smoke from the forge, disappeared. And Bud's three helpers stood around silently, waiting, staring at the newcomer.

"Is Bud here?" asked The Duke quietly.

There was no answer—nothing save those staring eyes fixed solemnly upon his face; and no one spoke. If things had come to such a pass as this, it was very bad indeed. He went on down the street with a faint smile still on his lips, but with desolation in his heart. They were all turned against him, every man of them, and the odds were crushing.

He went on without heeding where his footsteps were leading him until he stopped short with a start. Without his conscious volition he had turned from the main street and gone up a by-alley. Now he found himself squarely in front of the Murray house, and yonder was Mrs. Deacon, watering her hedge of sweet peas and watching—watch-

39

ing eagerly to see what he would do. And there was Mrs. Seth Murphy standing at her kitchen window and peering out. What should he do? He could not retreat now that he had come as far as this. So he turned in at the Murray gate. He climbed the steps. He tapped at the front door.

"Is that you, Bud?" called the voice of Linda from within.

He did not answer. There was a scurry of footsteps. The door was jerked open, and he found himself standing before the smiling, expectant girl. The smile went out at sight of him. She even jerked the door almost shut, but she opened it again on a crack and peered at him, a colorless and frightened face.

The Duke, removing his wide-brimmed sombrero, studied that face carefully. No matter how he himself had changed, the girl had altered even more. Or was he seeing the truth about her for the first time? It had never occurred to him in the old days that her eyes were a little close together or that her forehead was unnecessarily low or that her mouth was too generously wide. And certainly in three years the bloom was gone from her cheeks. She was the same—and yet she was entirely different. This was Linda, but he noted curiously that she did not affect him as he had expected she would. There was no sudden wrench and tearing at his heartstrings. It was as though he had picked a rose and raised it and found that the fragrance of the blossom was gone.

"Have you—have you—have you come to see me?" stammered Linda faintly.

"If you ain't too busy," said The Duke and smiled upon her.

Linda opened the door. She hesitated another moment.

"Will you come in—John?"

She had been almost the only person in the mountains who called him by his real name. The sound of it came sweetly home to him.

"I guess I'll stay here, Linda," he answered. "I just dropped around to give you a message."

"From whom?"

"From myself. I've come to tell you that Bud don't have to worry none about me. I went to see him and tell him the same thing, but I couldn't find him at his shop. I guess he had business some other place."

In spite of himself a faint sneer crept into his voice, and Linda colored hotly to the eyes.

"Bud ain't told me that he was worrying," she said.

"Is he keeping secrets from you already?" The Duke laughed.

He saw her wince under the acid of his irony.

"And, finally," he said, "I've come to wish you and Bud good luck."

He held out his hand. Slowly she put her own forth to meet it. He felt the tremor of her body as their fingers closed together, then fell apart.

"Oh, John," she was saying faintly, "it was such a long time, and people were saying such a lot of things—"

"Of course," said The Duke. "You couldn't wait forever."

"And we were so young," said Linda, half sobbing.

"We're older now," said The Duke. "We can see how foolish we were, Linda."

"I—yes," murmured Linda faintly

Certainly there was no joy in her voice. There was even a shade of wistfulness. Or so it seemed to The Duke.

He stepped back to the edge of the veranda.

"Good-bye, Linda."

"Good-bye, John."

He went down the street. He turned again at the gate and raised his hat to her once more. And was it not possible that the presence of the watchful ladies across the street made his smile even brighter than there was need as he turned away?

5

"Raised for an Outlaw"

BUT HE KNEW one thing with perfect surety as he went down the street again. Being free of Linda was like being free from deep sand when one wishes to ride fast. Being free from Linda was like coming from a hot lowland onto a breezy plateau. He put behind him the awakening from that old dream. If only he could have seen the truth about her three years before, how much happier that prison life would have been! As for Bud Springer, let him have all joy and happiness!

He went on to the verge of the town. It was not the same outer verge which he had known. Wheeler City had had a new lease of life and had spread outward rapidly during the past few years. But even the newcomers had heard of him. Doubtless the town paper had carried his picture during the past few days. Everyone was familiarized with the face of the "bad man." Yonder a stocky, dark-skinned little man who was hoeing in a vegetable garden stopped at his work and straightened to look at him with the wide and staring eyes to which The Duke was growing accustomed. He had heard all about the manslayer, and a faint dread of death was what made him stare so fixedly. And yonder was another he had never seen before, a buxom dame shrilling to her children and calling them in from the yard where they played. Now she gathered her two boys close to her and stared defiantly at the tall man in the street.

What did they take him to be—an ogre?

And yet there was an odd thrill about this. Better to be dreaded even by women and children than to be despised. Better to be like this than like Bud Springer, for instance, dodging out through the rear door of his shop when danger approached from the front. There was something fated about it. He had come home determined to live the life of a quiet and law-abiding man. But who could be quiet and law-abiding in such a murderous atmosphere of suspicion? If all their hands were to be against him, let his

44

hand, then, be against all other men! There was a charm in that dark and fatal future which fascinated him. In a little while, perhaps today or perhaps tomorrow, there was sure to be a crash. And afterward he would be an outlaw. As an outlaw he might maintain the battle for a few months, a few years, of skulking hither and thither, chilled by every rain and burned by every sun, wretched, lonely, supported in a desire to live only by the fierce joy of maintaining a single hand against the united force of society. And then a death, hunted down by numbers—a fighting death with his boots on!

Such was the force of these gloomy and exciting thoughts that he had slowed his walk and finally had halted with his head bowed. He did not raise it again until he heard the loud creaking of a heavy wagon in the near distance—and the jarring rattle of an empty wagonbed. He looked up in time to see the lead pair of a long team turn the corner, and span after span with nodding heads and the sagging traces which betokened an easy load or no load at all.

It was a huge freighter capable of supporting a burden of twenty thousand pounds over all the jarring rocks and the twisting ruts of the mountain roads. Its iron-spoked wheels rose as tall as a man. In front of it straggled seven couples of horses controlled by a jerkline from the driver on the lofty seat. The wrath of this driver was now aroused by the off horse in the sixes, a tall gray which must have stood a full sixteen two, and which was bucking and dancing and hurling itself from side to side with all its might. But it was helpless. Behind was the ponderous wagon on which, if necessary, the driver could jam the great brakes. And as for stepping to one side or the other, the weight and the strength of the horse ahead of him and of the horse beside him or the one behind him prevented. Yet he struggled like a mad creature, striving to draw back his head through the collar, then hurling himself forward as though bent on ripping his harness to bits. His gray coat was blackened with sweat, and bits of foam covered him.

The driver had been thrown into a paroxysm of fury, no doubt by the long continuance of the performance. Now he stood up in his place and swung the six-horse whip. In an amateur's hands that long stalk and that cumbersome, braided lash were worse than useless, and the lash was generally swung only to be curled around the neck of him who wielded it. But Tony Samatti was a man of another ilk. With all that length of stalk and lash it was said of Tony that he could swing and cut in two the horsefly on the hip of a horse without touching the hide of the horse. This was doubtless an exaggeration, but certain it was that he could wield his tremendous weapon with such force that it sliced through the hide as though there were a knife blade at work.

And he was plying the whip now, not with oaths but in a dreadful silence, his jaws locked, and the crack of the whip sending shivers through the rest of the team. They crouched and leaned anxiously into the collars, in dread lest their turn to taste fire should come next. And The Duke, lifting his fine head, walked around the leaders to get a better view of the punished horse.

He had had only a glimpse before. Now he could make sure that he had been right. The gray horse was far spent with exhaustion, but he was fighting with unabated vigor. In ten minutes more he would kill himself, and the dark-faced foreigner who drove would probably be glad to see him die.

Plainly this animal was a misfit. Aside from that one exception it was a splendidly balanced team. The leaders, well muscled but rangy enough for speed which leaders of a long team must have to keep the chain taut on a turn, might weigh twelve hundred or a shade less. The wheelers, solidly built, were a full fifteen hundred pounds apiece. And the spans between leaders and wheelers were carefully tapered. Yes, it was an ideal team —with the sole exception of this leggy gray stallion which was fighting against man and overruling destiny there ahead of the pointers. And what a horse that was! He had the agility of a panther and apparently the same savage temper. His legs were slenderly made; they were the legs of a runner, not a draft horse. His head short, small-muzzled, deep, from the eye to the point of the jaw, told of good blood. What was he doing in such a team as this?

The Duke held up his hand and Tony Samatti jammed on the brakes. They screamed, grated, and the wagon stopped. The team stood still, trembling even now in dread of the whip as Tony scrambled down from his seat. He abandoned the long whip. He came with a limber blacksnake in his hand.

The tall gray had stopped fighting and now stood shaking with nervous excitement and weariness—until the driver passed him. Then instantly there was another outbreak.

"Will you look at that long-legged fool?" queried Tony Samatti to the stranger, as the gray lunged and kicked and twisted against the harness. "I've handled hosses twenty years. I never seen the like of that—"

He finished the sentence with a rich profusion of oaths such as only a teamster has on the tip of his tongue for an emergency.

"Looks to me," said The Duke, "that the gray ain't up to the rest of your team, partner. Where'd you get him?"

"Up to the rest of the team? He ain't anywhere. He's crazy. How come I ain't taken him out of the traces and shot him to put him out of pain, I dunno. I got him in the foothills. Old Mike was my off hoss in the sixes. Never was a truer puller than Mike. He got took sudden with colic or something, gave about ten kicks and died on me. I hauled him downhill and stopped at the next ranch to get something to fill out that span. There was nobody but a widder woman at the ranch house. She showed me a pile of broncs about as high as my shoulder. Then she gave me a look at this gray off in a pasture by himself. Said her husband that had died a couple of months before had raised that hoss like a pet for four years and never had give him no work under anything but a saddle. Well, looked to me like he could fill out the team till we got to Wheeler City, and then I could sell him for something on account of his style. I gave her a hundred dollars cash and hitched him up. We went along a couple of miles till I started to make him pull, and then this here dance started and didn't come to no end. Raised for a pet? Raised for an outlaw, that's what he was raised for! Look out, stranger!"

The Duke had gone straight to the wild horse. The gray reared, plunged, strove to catch the newcomer with his teeth—and then suddenly was standing still and had nibbled something out of the outstretched palm of John Morrow.

"Now what in time have you got there?" asked the teamster in wonder, coming close.

"Sugar," said The Duke, and stepped back with that odd smile of his which had no mirth in it.

"Sugar?" echoed the driver, and he stared in utter bewilderment, for as The Duke turned his back the terrible gray stallion had crowded as close as he could get to him and now stared about his shoulder in defiance at